Lions!

Peter Millett
Jane Wallace-Mitchell

Australia • Brazil • Japan • Korea • Mexico • Singapore • Spain • United Kingdom • United States

Lions!

Fast Forward
Blue Level 11

Text: Peter Millett
Illustrations: Jane Wallace-Mitchell
Editor: Kate McGough
Design: Karen Mayo
Series design: James Lowe
Production controller: Emma Hayes
Reprint: Jennifer Foo
Audio recordings: Juliet Hill, Picture Start
Spoken by: Matthew King and Abbe Holmes

ISBN 978 0 17 012551 2
ISBN 978 0 17 012549 9 (set)

Cengage Learning Australia
Level 7, 80 Dorcas Street
South Melbourne, Victoria Australia 3205
Phone: 1300 790 853

Cengage Learning New Zealand
Unit 4B Rosedale Office Park
331 Rosedale Road, Albany, North Shore NZ 0632
Phone: 0800 449 725

For learning solutions, visit **cengage.com.au**

Printed in Australia by Ligare Pty Ltd
5 6 7 8 9 10 11 20 19 18 17 16

Evaluated in independent research by staff from the Department of Language, Literacy and Arts Education at the University of Melbourne.

Lions!

Peter Millett
Jane Wallace-Mitchell

Contents

Lions Everywhere

"Zac, look, there's a lion!"
shouted Thomas.

Zac looked to his right.
A lion walked in front of the truck.
"Cool. It looks really big,"
said Zac.

Thomas pointed behind the truck.
"Over there! There's another one."

Zac turned around.
"Do you think they are hunting us?"

"No," said Abasi.
"If a lion is hunting you,
you won't see it."

Zac pointed to his left as another lion
walked close to the truck.
"They look *really* hungry."

Thomas reached for his camera.
Suddenly, he and Zac
were rocked to the floor.
The truck stopped.

"Are you okay, Zac?" said Thomas.

"Yes, I'm okay," said Zac.

Zac and Thomas got up.

"What happened?" said Thomas.

Problems

Abasi leaned over the roof of the truck and shouted down to his father.

His father pointed at the engine. Steam was coming out of it.

"We have a problem," said Abasi.

Thomas and Zac looked at each other.

"Can your father fix the problem?" said Thomas.

"I hope so," said Abasi.

Running Words 166

"I hope so, too," said Zac
as he looked around at the lions.

Thomas and Zac waited quietly
for Abasi's father
to start the engine again.

Thomas saw another lion
come out of the bush.
"Are we safe up here, Abasi?" he said.

"Yes, you are safe up here," said Abasi.
"But if you step out there,
you won't be safe."

Getting Late

It was getting late in the day.
Abasi's father tried to start
the engine again,
but it just wouldn't go.
Now, Zac and Thomas were afraid.

Suddenly, Zac shouted:
"Hey, I can't see the lions anywhere!"

Thomas looked left and right.
"Where have they gone?" he shouted.

Abasi looked over
at the bush.
He saw
a big shadow
move quickly.
He looked to his left
and saw
another big shadow
moving behind it.

"Father!" he shouted,
banging on the truck.

Safe

Abasi's father tried to start the engine again.
The engine was cool now.

"Father! Lions!" shouted Abasi.

Suddenly, the engine started.
Abasi's father put his foot down and took off.
Thomas and Zac looked behind at the lions.

"I was sure the lions were hunting us," said Zac.

Abasi laughed.
"No, no!
The lions would not want to eat you two.
You boys are too skinny for them," he laughed.

Zac and Thomas laughed, too.